For the creatures of the hundred-acre woods
I'm lucky enough to share
—M. J. R.

For my family, John and Pat
—A.W.

Text copyright © 2019 by Michael J. Rosen
Jacket art and interior illustrations copyright © 2019 by Annie Won

All rights reserved. Published in the United States by Doubleday, an imprint of
Random House Children's Books, a division of Penguin Random House LLC, New York.

Doubleday and the colophon are registered trademarks of Penguin Random House LLC.

Visit us on the Web! rhcbooks.com

Educators and librarians, for a variety of teaching tools, visit us at RHTeachersLibrarians.com

Library of Congress Cataloging-in-Publication Data
Names: Rosen, Michael J., author. | Won, Annie, illustrator.
Title: In the quiet, noisy woods / by Michael J. Rosen ; illustrated by Annie Won.
Description: First edition. | New York : Doubleday, [2019]
Summary: A forest's quiet chorus of chirps, clicks, and chits changes to loud scree-scree-screeches
and other noises as two rambunctious wolf pups, separated from their pack, scamper and chase.
Identifiers: LCCN 2017060555 (print) | LCCN 2018004233 (ebook)
ISBN 978-1-5247-6665-8 (hc) | ISBN 978-1-5247-6666-5 (glb) | ISBN 978-1-5247-6667-2 (ebook)
Subjects: | CYAC: Animal sounds—Fiction. | Forest animals—Fiction. | Forests and forestry—Fiction. |
Wolves—Fiction. | Animals—Infancy—Fiction.
Classification: LCC PZ7.R71868 (ebook) | LCC PZ7.R71868 In 2019 (print) | DDC [E]—dc23

MANUFACTURED IN CHINA
10 9 8 7 6 5 4 3 2 1
First Edition

In the Quiet NOISY Woods

Michael J. Rosen

illustrated by Annie Won

Autumn
Christmas
2019

Michael
J. Rosen
2019

Doubleday Books for Young Readers

Into the quiet noise of the woods—the all-day, everywhere chorus of *chirp*s and *click*s and *chit*s that peep and repeat . . .

Who's there?

Over here, over here.

Stay away!

You there?

Feed me! Feed me!

That's mine!

All's well . . .

Who's there?

Over here, over here.

Stay away!

You there?

Feed me! Feed me!

That's mine!

All's well . . .

. . . into these quiet, noisy woods,
a wolf pup *yip-yap-yowls*
as she bounds over a limb from a birch
and bursts through the brambles and wildflowers,

yip-yap

chasing her *grr-ruff-ruff-racing* brother,
who scampers along a shallow stream,
then dashes in a tight circle to return the chase.

grr-ruff-ruff

chit-chitter

A pair of squirrels plucking acorns under an oak skedaddle up the tree, *chit-chitter*-chattering about a *yip-yap*-yowling wolf chasing another *grr-ruff-ruff*-racing wolf who is splish-splashing along the stream that trickles through their quiet, noisy woods.

Chick-a-dee, chick-a-dee-dee-dee, warns a black-capped chickadee who's weaving moss into a grassy nest when she hears the squirrels' *chit-chitter*-chatter about the *yip-yap*-yowling wolf pup and her *grr-ruff-ruff*-racing brother, splashing and dashing through their forest.

chick-a-dee, chick-a-dee-dee-dee

A turkey, nestled atop her clutch of eggs, suddenly *fwap-fwap-flaps* her wings when the chickadee's *chick-a-dee, chick-a-dee-dee-dee* and the squirrels' *chit-chitter*-chatter tell her about the *yip-yap-yowling, grr-ruff-ruff-racing* pups playing wolf tag in their quiet, noisy woods.

fwap-fwap

A fox *swoosh-whoosh*-rushes out of her den, alarmed
by the *fwap-fwap*-flaps of the turkey who heard the chickadee's
chick-a-dee, chick-a-dee-dee-dee about the squirrels'
chit-chitter-chattering because the *yip-yap*-yowling
wolf pup and the *grr-ruff-ruff*-racing wolf pup were chasing
each other while their pack dozed in the midday sunshine.

swoosh-whoosh

Beside four dozing fawns, a watchful buck *stomp-stomp*-stamps
when he smells the *swoosh-whoosh*-rushing fox
who saw the *fwap-fwap*-flapping turkey who heard
the chickadee's *chick-a-dee, chick-a-dee-dee-dee* warning
because the squirrels' *chit-chitter*-chatter meant
that two *yip-yap*-yowling, *grr-ruff-ruff*-racing wolf pups
were not with the rest of the pack in the field.

stomp-stomp

Peck, nip, pick—three mourning doves *whift-wish*-whistle
and lift from the ground when the buck *stomp-stomp*-stamps
because he caught the scent of the *swoosh-whoosh*-rushing fox

who noticed the turkey's *fwap-fwap*-flaps after
the chickadee's *chick-a-dee, chick-a-dee-dee-dee*
call about the squirrels' *chit-chitter*-chattering
because the *yip-yap*-yowling, *grr-ruff-ruff*-racing
pups are splashing and tumbling and playing
in their quiet and noisy woods.

whift-wish

scree-scree

Alerted by the ruckus, a hawk *scree-scree*-screeches
and dives into the much less quiet woods
where the mourning doves *whift-wish*-whistled
because the buck *stomp-stomp*-stamped
when the fox *swoosh-whoosh*-rushed
past after the turkey *fwap-fwap*-flapped
because the chickadee called *chick-a-dee, chick-a-dee-dee-dee*
since the *chit-chitter*-chattering squirrels announced a *yip-yap*-yowling
and a *grr-ruff-ruff*-racing pair of wolf pups separated from their pack.

stomp-stomp

chick-a-dee, chick-a-dee-dee-dee

fwap-fwap

chit-chitter

Above all the sounds in these not-at-all-quiet
and suddenly very noisy woods—

scree-screeeeee

swoosh-whoosh

whift-wish

from not-so-far-away,
there's a single long, loud . . .

grr-ruff-ruff

yip-yap

wuff-wuff-wa-o o o o o o o o o ooooooooooooooooooooo

grr-ruff-ruff-aw-oooooooo

It's the howl of the wolf pups' father:
Where are you two?
And then there's a second howl: their mother adding
her own *grr-grr-growl* and *yip-yap-yowl*.
Get back here now!

OOOOOO!

arf-arf-ruff-ruff-oooooo-arf-ruff-ruff!

The two pups stop their chasing,
crane their necks skyward,
and bark their answer:

yip-yip-yippeeeeee! grr-row-row! row-row!

We're coming! Be right there!

And now the voices of seven wolves—
the whole family—fill the woods
with whines and yodels and laughs
and huffs and growls and barks.
It's a song of greeting.
A song of reunion.
A family song.

woo-oo-wow

wuff-wuff-wa-o o o o o o o o o oooo

rarr-rarr-ooo-reeeeeeeeee

yip-yip-yip
yip-yip-yip

yow-yow

yuk-yuk-ha-ha-ha

OOOOOOOOOOOOOOOO

aw-ruff-ruff-a-roooooo

hah-wooooooo-
wow-eeeeeee

snuff-huff

grr-ruff-ruff-aw-o o o o o o arf-arf-ruff-ruff-oooooo

ha-ooooooooooooooo

And then, just as suddenly, the wolves' song is over.

The squirrels return to plucking acorns

and the chickadee weaves moss into her grassy nest

and the turkey nestles atop her clutch of eggs

and the fox grooms her kits inside their den

and the deer are ready to doze once more

and the mourning doves settle on the ground to feed

and the hawk glides far from the quiet, noisy woods where,

once again, you can hear the all-day, everywhere chorus

of *chirps* and *clicks* and *chits* that peep and repeat. . . .

Who's there?

Over here, over here.

Stay away!

You there?

Feed me! Feed me!

That's mine!

All's well?

All's well.

Get to Know These Quiet, Noisy Creatures

Wolf

You might say a wolf looks like a large herding or sled-pulling dog. That's because modern dogs descended from wolves.

Once, wolves inhabited much of North America. But hunting reduced their numbers severely. Today, these predators are still endangered.

Each spring, adult females give birth to several pups. Weak and helpless, the newborns live with their mother and father and sometimes a few youngsters from the previous year's litter in an underground den. About ten months later, now fully able to fend for themselves, the pups leave.

Wolves hunt together over a large territory, so communication is key! Their huffs, yelps, whines, barks, and howls—especially at night, when they're most active—keep the pack together.

Squirrel

You've probably heard a squirrel chitter-chattering as it leaps among tree branches or scampers across a phone line. Some two hundred kinds of squirrels can be found in cities and parks on every continent except Antarctica and Australia.

Do you know that squirrels hide extra food? They tuck away acorns and other nuts in secret places every summer and fall, and then, searching in winter, they remember where most are stored! And because squirrels' front teeth get worn down by the hard foods they eat, the teeth keep growing throughout their lives. A squirrel's teeth might grow six inches in a year!

Chickadee

This common songbird, found in all seasons throughout most of North America, is a favorite at bird feeders, often hanging upside down to peck at seeds.

Chickadees tend to flock in small groups, flitting among leafy limbs, cheerily calling their own name: *chick-a-dee, chick-a-dee-dee-dee*. While they do nab insects in flight, they mostly bop between branches, feeding on spiders, caterpillars, and berries.

If you see a chickadee flying off again and again with a single sunflower seed in its beak, you may wonder: How can such a small bird eat so much? In fact, it's tucking the seeds away for winter eating.

Wild Turkey

You might know something of the wild turkey if you've ever drawn a bird by tracing the outline of your flattened hand. Your thumb is the neck and head; your other fingers, the plumes of its fanned tail.

These large, plump birds are found in wooded areas throughout the United States (except Alaska), as well as in parts of Canada and Central America. They travel in flocks, scraping their feet across the ground to find insects and also feeding on nuts, seeds, ferns, and berries. While they form simple nests on the ground with whatever grasses, leaves, and sticks might be present, they roost among a tree's branches to sleep.

AMERICAN MUSEUM
OF NATURAL HISTORY

STERLING CHILDREN'S BOOKS
New York

An Imprint of Sterling Publishing Co., Inc.
1166 Avenue of the Americas
New York, NY 10036

ISBN 978-1-4549-2237-7

Distributed in Canada by Sterling Publishing Co., Inc.
c/o Canadian Manda Group, 664 Annette Street
Toronto, Ontario, Canada M6S 2C8
Distributed in the United Kingdom by GMC Distribution Services
Castle Place, 166 High Street, Lewes, East Sussex, England BN7 1XU
Distributed in Australia by NewSouth Books
45 Beach Street, Coogee, NSW 2034, Australia

For information about custom editions, special sales, and premium and corporate purchases,
please contact Sterling Special Sales at 800-805-5489 or specialsales@sterlingpublishing.com.

Manufactured in China

Lot #:
2 4 6 8 10 9 7 5 3 1
03/17

www.sterlingpublishing.com

Jacket and interior design by Sharon Jacobs

IMAGE CREDITS

AnimalsAnimals © Robert Winslow: 25; **Alamy** © Morgan Wildlife: 27, © Debbie Steinhausser: 16; **Getty Images** © Jim Austin/Jimages Digital Photography:
front cover, © Jim Cumming: 9, © James Hager/Robert Harding: 12, © Thomas Kitchin & Victoria Hurst: 17 (top), © Alexandru Magurean: 13, © Oxford Scientific: 6,
© Tambako the Jaguar: 7 (top), © Tier Und Naturfotografie J und C Sohns: 17 (bottom), © Michael Weber: 23, 30–31, © Ronald Wittek: 10; **iStockphoto** © Andyworks: 11,
26, © Johny87: 28–29, © Kjekol: endpapers, 24, © Ramiro Marquez Photos: 22 (bottom); **Kimball Stock** © Klein-Hubert: 20–21; **Minden Pictures** © Jim Brandenburg:
2–3, 18, back cover, © Tim Fitzharris: 5, © Klein and Hubert: 8, © Konrad Wothe: 14–15; **Shutterstock** © LesPalenik: 7 (bottom); © **Robert Winslow**: 22 (top)

AMERICAN MUSEUM ᴼᶠ NATURAL HISTORY

Wolf Pups Join the Pack

STERLING CHILDREN'S BOOKS

New York

On a sunny spring day, a litter of baby wolves is born. Baby wolves are called pups. Wolf pups will stay in the den until they are ready to join other wolves.

At five weeks old, wolf pups are full of energy! They spend more time outside the den and are curious about the world. There is so much to explore!

But wolf pups can't roam very far on their own. They are small and rely on their parents and other adult wolves for food and protection.

Before they can eat solid food, wolf pups drink their mother's milk. Pups nurse four to five times a day. Their mother's milk gives them the nutrients they need to grow.

Pups are the newest members of the wolf family.

A wolf family is called a pack.

Not all packs are the same—they differ in size. Some are large and have many wolves, while others are small with only a few.

The parents of wolf pups leave the pack to go hunting. Sometimes, other adult wolves will stay behind to make sure the pups are safe and cared for.

The mother and father may be gone for many days, searching for food to bring home. When they return, they are greeted with lots of licks on the face.

At nine weeks old, wolf pups have teeth. They begin to eat solid food but still need help. A parent or another adult wolf eats the food first and then spits it back up for the pups.

Wolves mostly eat meat, such as deer, elk, and moose. They don't always eat every day. When there is not enough food available, wolves can go days without eating.

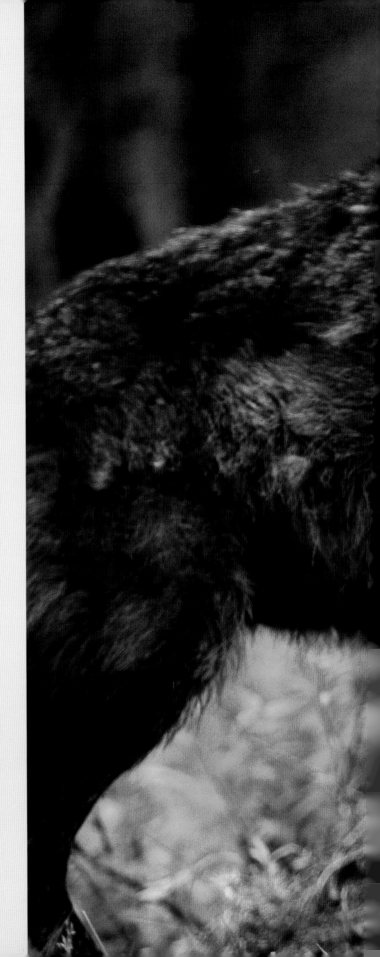

When summer comes around, the pups start picking up useful skills. They practice hunting and stalking prey. They are becoming more independent.

The pups grow bigger
and bigger each day—
and they have just as
much energy as before!
They run and wrestle
under the summer sun.

Whenever adult wolves and their pups are separated, they talk to each other by howling. "Owwhooooo!" a wolf howls, sticking her nose in the air.

A wolf pup hears the call and answers with a howl of his own.

He lifts his head. His ears go back. He takes a deep breath.

"Owwhoooo!"

By the time fall arrives, the pups have grown strong. They are able to run quickly—fast enough to keep up with the older wolves! They start running as part of the pack.

Before long, it starts to get colder. Fall turns into winter. The ground is covered in a thick blanket of snow. The pups are nine months old and are not considered pups anymore.

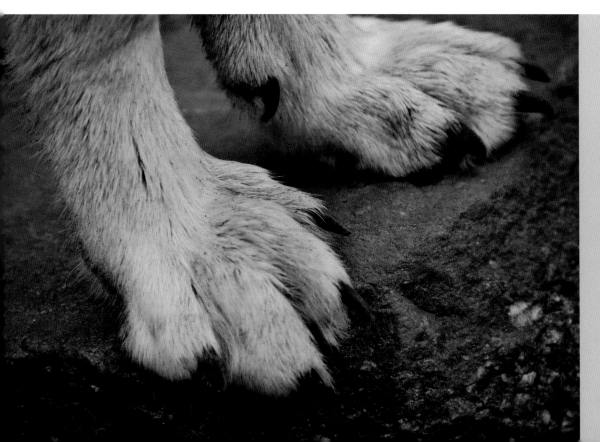

They are now young wolves. Young wolves have large feet and sharp claws. This helps them run across icy surfaces.

Young wolves do not rely on others for food.

They hunt on their own for small animals.

To catch large animals, they hunt as a team with the rest of the pack.

All that running around can be exhausting!

Young wolves need to rest every now and then.

They curl up in a ball. Their thick fur keeps them warm as they drift into a deep sleep.

When they grow older, some wolves will leave the pack, while others will stay. But until then, the young wolves stick together.

Meet the Expert

My name is **Neil Duncan**, and I am a biologist. I work for the Department of Mammalogy at the American Museum of Natural History in New York City. As the collections manager, I get to work with all kinds of animal specimens that have been gathered from around the world.

The natural world has always been a passion of mine, and I have traveled all over the world to study animals. In California, I researched small forest carnivores called fishers and martens. In the Bahamas, Belize, and Papua New Guinea, I worked alongside other biologists surveying the biodiversity of those areas. Currently, I am involved with the Gotham Coyote Project, studying coyotes as they expand their range throughout the boroughs of New York City and into Long Island, where I grew up.